A catalogue record for this book is available from the British Library
Published by Ladybird Books Ltd
80 Strand London WC2R ORL
A Penguin Company

1 3 5 7 9 10 8 6 4 2

© LADYBIRD BOOKS LTD MMIV

Animal Stories

Muddy Molly

written by Ronne Randall

illustrated by John Haslam

Ladybird

Deep in the jungle, there was a winding, wandering river. It was the glubbiest, blubbiest, MUDDIEST river anywhere.

Perfect for hippos!

mud-paddle...

and even deep-mud diving!

No matter how hot and steamy
the jungle was, the mud was always
nice and cool.

In fact, the only things that ever made the hippos hot were the buzzing, nipping insects that flew around the river.

Luckily for the hippos, the friendly birds who lived around the river thought the insects were delicious. Each bird chose its favourite hippo and sat on its back quietly feasting on bugs and flies.

So most of the hippos were very happy. All except one.

Poor Molly didn't have her own bird friend to eat up all the bugs!

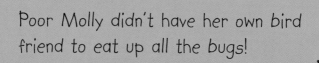

"This buzzing

and biting and itching

and twitching is driving me mad!" said Molly. "I'll have to find a friend of my own!"

So Molly set off up the river.
Soon, she met Crocodile.
"Hello, Molly," said Crocodile, snapping
his shiny white teeth. "I'll help you to
get rid of those biting bugs!"

"No, thanks," said Molly,
swimming past as fast as she could.

Molly swam further up the river.
"Hello, Molly!" shouted Roaring Rory and
Stripey Sam. "We'll help you to swish
those nasty flies away with our tails!"

"No, thanks," said Molly, swimming quickly by.

Soon, Molly was in a part of the jungle she'd never seen before. She was a little bit scared.

"Maybe I'd better go home, before I get lost," she thought.

But, suddenly, Molly heard something in the trees. It was a little bird.

Molly waved to the bird, and the bird fluttered down and settled on her tummy. The bird picked and pecked hungrily, and soon all the bugs were gone!

Before long, Molly was swimming happily home with her new friend on her back.

"No more itching or twitching!" thought Molly. "Thank you, Little Bird!"

"Tweet!" cheeped Little Bird.

"Welcome home, Molly!" called her friends. "We thought you were lost. Where have you been?"

"I've been all the way up the river," said Molly. "And I've found a new friend."

"Tweet!" said Little Bird.

Molly knew what that meant...

She had her own special bird friend at last. And no more itches!